MW00979170

RED

COLORS: CHAPTER I

TYLER VO

Parental Advisory: Explicit Content (mature language and graphic content)

At the center of it all there was love.

Copyright © 2020 by Tyler Vo
All rights reserved. This book or any portion thereof
may not be reproduced or used in any manner
whatsoever without the express written permission of
the publisher except for the use of brief quotations in
a book review.

ISBN 978-1-6502-3458-8

Dear Reader,

You may not know me very well, or perhaps you are one of my good friends. Regardless, I just wanted to thank you for opening my book and taking the time out of your day to read my writing. It hasn't always been easy for me to be so open and vulnerable with my writing. Writing used to be something so private and closed off for me. It was my security blanket and helped me express myself while I outwardly donned a mask of inexpression and stoic. However, knowing that there are people such as yourself out there who are not only interested in the words I print on these pages, but also are willing to take a risk and allow yourself to consume my material emboldens me to continue sharing the art that I've come to adore so much. I've said it many times before and I'll continue saying it until it's no longer true but writing saved my life many years ago. It kept me from self-harming and it opened up a pathway for me to let the pen bleed in my place. Now to be completely honest, I didn't start writing for an audience. I never imagined I would actually have any semblance of the reach I currently have. I never thought that having people actually want to read my writing was something I wanted. I don't know what I want to do in the future with my writing or where I plan on taking it. But just 4 years ago I would have never imagined having two independently published books and a third one on the way just over the horizon. You, the reader, inspire, motivate, and drive me to constantly push myself to expand my creative boundaries and produce works of art that provoke thought and emotion and give you a small piece of me. So, I thank you for taking this ride with me. Whether you've been following my writing from middle school when I thought I was going to be a rapper or if you just recently read my published works, I wholeheartedly appreciate the support. There's a lot more writing and exciting projects coming very soon so stay patient and be ready.

Your humble raconteur,
        Tyler Vo

BLOOD
9

WAR
13

LOVE
34

DANGER
39

ROSE
77

WARMTH
79

Blood

Macabre, family, sacrifice, harm, death. These are just a few of the topics that can be tied to blood in one way or another that interest me, especially in writing. Blood's texture and crimson color are both haunting and gorgeous to me at the same time. The way it seeps and spreads unlike any other liquid is profound and offers such a chilling yet mesmerizing image. The contrast between the sanguine tint of blood and a white canvas paints blood as an extravagant stain on an otherwise pristine surface. That stark juxtaposition of life and death through the very thing that encapsulates life itself has been an area of captivation for me. I wanted to be able to draw out the comparison between our human lifeline and purity as an innate conflict rather than a symbiotic correlation.

and away we go

We often think of death as a cruel robbery of life
But I've come to know the Reaper as a companion.
One who protects me from the screeching darkness
And the boundless pain of drawing breath after
breath;
My mind is at its most peaceful when my heart
slows almost to a halt,
Close enough to death and its reassuring hands.
As I walk forward into the shadowy night
The evening chill sends ripples of tumultuous
serenity
In phase with every beating palpitation in my
hollow chest
For the ethereal blanket of space wraps itself around
my visage
Shielding me from that devastating celestial light
And tucking me in to the eternal sleep.
Forgive me for wasting your time with my futile
efforts,
Abysmal appeals to empathy and emotion,
Disorderly behavior, and unbecoming spite;
Because I only wanted to spare you the loss
But now I understand the burden of loving someone
Who refuses to adorn their life with such pure,
unadulterated care
As you have placed upon me unwarranted and
unconditionally.
We'll leave the bench we've been sitting on forever
And you'll grace the familiar road back home.
I'll watch you disappear around the bend
Before I look down at my bloodied wrists,
Their scars opened wide enough for the rivers to run
dry
Covering the cement with our story
As history forgets my name.

Recovery

My mind wanders further than my body
Leaving my heart trailing in the wind as it glides up
the harrowing road ahead.
We choose to forget but I'm quite fond of the past.
My memories are my greatest treasures.
They remind me of the bitterness of grasping
unsuccessfully at happiness and the tantalizing
inability to hold on to security and familiarity.
As I stumble through the hallways illuminated with
flickering lights
Distorting my vision with their dim radiation,
I hear the bellowing screams of night terrors
yearning to break out into the daylight-
Their sick, morose songs echo unfiltered along the
hospital walls.
My assistant smiles grimly as he feels my muscles
tense as he guides me to my office.
I crash through the door and fall violently to my
knees.
Today is not the day my assistant utters stoically.
I begin to weep
I pick at the cold floor beneath me
I begin to scream.
I writhe back and forth on the ground and respond
to the calls of the ghouls next door with a screeching
laughter.
I can feel my arms begin to free and my strength
return to me.
My amusement turns sinister as I glance back up at
the door:
My assistant stood there frozen with his mouth
agape-
Before he could turn away or say his last words my
hand swung at his throat and his lifeless body
dropped to the floor.

Sanguine blood soaked my pale nightgown as I trudged over the corpse and out into the light.
We choose to forget but I never have.
I live with my demons and tonight I'm letting them out.

War

Conflict is an everlasting facet of our lives whether we experience it daily or ever so often. It could be within ourselves internally or with our surroundings, but it tests our patience, emotional stability, and decision making amongst other things. However, seldom times do we feel at war with an entity or being in our lives. War is exhausting. War is destructive. War is successive. Throughout history, large battles and political decisions tend to steal the spotlight from the totality of wars but it is the conglomeration of these dominoes falling that paint the larger picture of war's expense on all parties involved. The damage done is not always worn by either side. Sometimes winners are left worse off, wondering at what cost did achieving victory bring. There are no true victors in war. I've been dealing with conflict, mostly internal, my whole life but my early adulthood and beyond has been largely defined by my inexpression of outward emotion. I wear smiles like a mask and people are often surprised when they get to catch glimpses of the darkness and torrential downpour I harbor inside. So, I wrote this personal blog-like narrative so you can understand what it's like To Be Me.

To Be Me

I never had a strong relationship with my parents. Ever since I was young I clashed with my father more times than I could consciously remember before the age of nine, and I never truly could tell if I comprehended what love was. Sure, my parents told me almost every day that they loved me before school or before bed, but I didn't feel that warmth or tender comfort in their words like I had seen portrayed in media and with my friends' families. I'm pretty sure I loved both of my parents even as a child, but I was scared of them more than I could convince myself I loved them.

I guess I should start by providing some context and insight into who my family is. Both of my parents (and my grandparents on my mother's side who have lived with me since I was four months old) are refugees from the Vietnam War and emigrated to America when they were roughly twenty years old. My father grew up in the suburbs of Saigon where he was raised in very humble conditions and his family definitely had their fair share of struggles while he was growing up. My mother, on the other hand, was born in a small village called Quang Ngai in the central region of the country and moved to Saigon a while later while still a young child. She was the only surviving child of my two grandparents and lived a much more comfortable life than my father did. I don't know much about their lives before America, but I do know that their lives changed forever when the Viet Cong attacked, forcing them to flee their homes and move to the United States.

So yeah, my parents were never comfortable living like a nuclear American family; they never needed to and there was nothing inherently wrong with that. But they picked Huntington Beach, California out of all places to raise our family: a coastal surfer's paradise densely populated with conservative white Americans. Thus, I grew up in a quintessentially traditional Vietnamese household in the middle of a community of well-off white people. Growing up, this was the only reality I knew, and I never felt out of my element or uncomfortable with my surroundings. Most of my friends were white and most of the people I saw on a daily basis were white. I accepted this as simply the way life works in America.

Stop me if you've heard this before, but I existed in a whole different world than my parents. As a first generation Asian American growing up in Huntington Beach and raised by traditional immigrant parents, I enjoyed a unique blend of cultures from an early age. My first language was Vietnamese. My earliest favorite foods and games were American. The majority of my classmates were white. My teachers were almost all white. I played the holy trinity of American sports growing up: basketball, baseball and football. When I was younger I used to not know there was a distinction between being Asian American and just American. What a blissfully ignorant time. As I got older, I became fluent in Vietnamese, understood the cultural values of my heritage, and adored the irreplaceable value of having grown up learning how to navigate both American and Vietnamese walks of life simultaneously.

There was a time in my life, however, in which I rejected my Asian, and by extension my Vietnamese, upbringing because I despised how other first generation Asian American kids at school and in public acted. They were so adamant about wanting to be defined by their "Asian" traits and interests, yet very obviously had no genuine understanding or connection to their cultural roots. Most of them could barely speak their native language, if at all. They celebrated their respective Asian holidays only when it was convenient for them and knew nothing about the history of their own countries. However, they loved feeding into white people's stereotypes of what Asians like to do as if that validated their "Asian" identity. It probably angered me way more than necessary but at its worst I was disgusted and had no desire to be associated with that community anymore. Thus, while I was in high school I began to hang out with white people more and tried as best I could to disassociate myself from the other Asian American students.

This phase of my life is particularly embarrassing to me in retrospect because I should have never allowed such minor transgressions by other irrelevant people dictate my acceptance of my family's background. I let my repressed desire to be accepted and viewed favorably by the popular white kids at school convince myself, at least for a short while, that it might have been better to be seen as a whitewashed Asian than a stereotypical Asian in their eyes. Turns out, it didn't matter anyways. A double edged sword to my ego, the popular kids never cared that I was Asian but at the same time I was also one of the very few Asian kids that regularly hung out with them, in essence becoming a token one. I never imagined that I would voluntarily be the token Asian in any setting, considering I refused to self-identify as anything other than simply American at the time.

It shouldn't be a surprise that my conflicts with my parents escalated and erupted violently very quickly during that same time period in high school. I wrote my first book about the consequences of the deterioration of my relationship with my parents when I was 16. You can read more about that whole ordeal by ordering my book on lulu.com by searching "35 Days Tyler Vo" in the search bar on the homepage. Go get it now if you haven't already. Seriously, go.

Long story (read "very short, self-published memoir") short, my disagreements with my parents concerning my lifestyle choices led to us mutually burning bridges with one another at the time. Obviously, my parents weren't going to leave so I packed my bags and left for 35 days. If I had to do it all over again, I wouldn't have left. Not for anything.

But that was almost six years ago. A lot has

changed since then. I actively worked on repairing and rebuilding my relationship with my parents throughout my four years in college and currently have a relatively healthy relationship with both of them. I've finally allowed myself to trust them and am extremely appreciative of their support and help in everything I've been blessed to do, and I surely hope they feel as if they can trust me as well. It definitely feels like it. But as one conflict resolves, another one rises from the ashes.

My Phoenix is self-doubt and self-hatred. While I've been investing my time and energy into making peace with my family, my own demons have gone to war with my sanity and happiness. I have always been my harshest critic and whether or not that has kept me humble to a degree throughout the years, it also impedes my sense of self-worth and fulfillment. From as far back as I can remember, I could never muster the courage to accept myself and my insecurities commanded every aspect of my life. Whether it be in personal appearance, acceptance from others, or internal dissatisfaction with my soul, there has never been a shortage of internal struggle for control of my mind between my vulnerabilities and my confidence.

Let's start with body dysmorphia. As a very young child, I was healthy and not under or overweight in any way. Around the end of elementary school, I began to fill out a little bit, and by the seventh grade or so, I was overweight. A lot of my clothes stopped fitting and I began to wear outfits that would mask how round my figure was becoming. This included always wearing sweatshirts and jackets even when it was scalding hot outside as well as only sporting looser fitting jeans and pants. Maybe the pants were for the better anyways since this was the "skinny jeans and vans" era of fashion and let me tell you, I never really regretted not being able to take part in that trend (shouts out Lil Wayne for popularizing the trend for the culture though).

This self-perception of becoming fat and

overweight was not strictly internalized either. Every part of my life reminded me of the fact that I was gaining weight. I got teased at school about my stomach by some of the older kids in the locker room while I was changing for PE. My basketball coach of the travel team I played for at the time singled out my stomach and weight as a primary reason why I was losing playing time on the court; my poor conditioning was hindering my ability to keep up with quicker players.

I remember having to shop for new pants for my piano competitions with my mom one afternoon. That was the first time I ever paid attention to waist sizes on pants. I tried on so many pairs of pants that day; there was always something that couldn't fit well whether it be too tight at the waist or on my legs. Finally, my mom found a pair with adjustable waist sizes ranging from 28-36 that was labeled as "husky fit" for the legs. I put the pants on and they fit comfortably around my legs, but the waistline needed adjusting so I loosened the waist until I found the preset size that would allow me to breathe without sagging. I took a look down at the winning choice: 34. I was a size 34 waist at the age of 12 years old. My mom laughed at me when I walked out of the changing room and told her which size fit me best. My brother and sister joined in and were in awe of how big I had become. Coming to terms with a number that could quantify just how fat I knew everyone around me could see I had become was gut wrenching.

That memory has been seared into the deepest recesses of my mind for 10 years now. I remember every detail of that day with such vivid clarity it astonishes me that it was almost half a lifetime ago. That one miserable day set off a chain of events and choices that continue to guide me to this day. First, I starved myself throughout the rest of middle school. I never packed a lunch and told my mom I would be buying food at school but instead would just skip eating and sleep during lunchtime. Not surprisingly, my first serious attempts at self-harm occurred around this time. This practice would continue into the first couple years of high school as well. In college I eventually became very strict with my diet and tried to be as meticulous as possible with what I chose to eat.

Fast forward to today and I've only very recently been able to convince myself that I've changed my body type for the healthier. While in no way do I think I am perfectly healthy or some motivational success story, I don't plan on experiencing the same trauma that got me here ever again. I made a vow that same day 10 years ago to improve my health and never let myself get anywhere near that point ever again. I constantly relive the agonizing and seemingly endless misery that plagued my adolescent mind by replaying over and over again all the episodes in the past of friends and family constantly reminding me about how fat I'd become. That pain, that devastating confrontation with reality is what I battle with in my heart to keep myself moving forward every day.

In addition to my ever evolving body image insecurities, I've struggled immensely with seeking acceptance from others, and by extension myself, as validation for my successes. Notice how I specifically said "successes" and not something trivial like social status or something even more tragic like personality (seriously, just imagine how sad that would be). I never gave more of a (bad word) than the average Joe about what people thought about me as a person or whether or not they liked me. A different kind of self-doubt haunts me: not being or doing enough. There isn't a specific time in my life I could point to as the moment when I was able to convince myself I was special, but I know it happened at an early age.

I fondly remember the first word used to describe me in a unique way was "observant." My mom loved to remind me how extremely observant I was when I was very young. I didn't know what I had said or done that was noticeable for my mom to say that and I still don't. I was just being curious. I still am. But you see, that's kind of what has troubled, and perhaps hindered, me my whole life. Throughout every phase or chapter of my life, I've been handed a bigger and bigger part of the world and told to do something great with it. Almost all the greats in any walk of life tend to understand and realize their greatness and that's what empowers them to meet and exceed the gargantuan expectations thrust upon their shoulders. So why on Earth did the universe decide that I should be one to burden such great expectations? I never asked to be great, nor did I ever assume I would be; that's essentially the problem.

When you are constantly told from the age of five all the way through college that you are going to do amazing things and change the world, you tend to convince yourself that you are somehow destined to fit this mold people have built for you your entire life even if it seems incredibly far-fetched. Someone once told me that the name "Tyler Vo" meant something powerful to a lot of different people. My name…? My NAME? What the hell does that even mean? I never knew what to do with these lofty expectations people around me wanted me to live up to, so I eventually came to believe that I was indeed worthy of such high praises because I honestly do have the capability to be great.

But in truth? I am so scared. Scared that I won't ever be able to accomplish enough to satisfy the goals I have set for myself. Failure looms over the horizon with everything I set out to achieve and its foreboding presence reminds me that I am mortal. But at this point I don't want to be mortal. The only thing that drives me forward and keeps my heart beating is my desire to positively impact as many lives as possible, and thus changing the world for the better. This is my only life goal and quite frankly the only thing that gives me purpose. And to that point, what happens when I can't do enough to impact the world? How many lives is enough? Will I ever be able to tell myself I did the most I could do? What happens when I can't accomplish the most important thing I set out to do? If I fail to realize the one thing that gives me purpose, did I lead a meaningless life?

I don't have the answers. I never did. I understand that as I get older people care less about what I'm doing with my life. They have their own stresses and worries. But I've developed a pseudo God complex that constantly tells me if I can't be some sort of superhero then I am not deserving of my life. There's been nothing to suggest I need to become one or am even capable of it but nonetheless it's deeply ingrained in my psychology at this point. I have formed an unhealthy obsession with attaining an ultimately unrealizable goal and perhaps that's what eternally minimizes my satisfaction with my life.

I often wish that I could have went through my formative years without anybody noticing me. Just slipping under the radar without people thinking I was capable of anything special.

Perhaps I would have spent more time pursuing things that brought me joy instead of worrying about whether or not I was putting myself in the right position to be some sort of hero sometime down the road. Now I'm 22 with no real understanding of what I'm supposed to do or sense of direction. Being "Tyler Vo" isn't as peachy as it used to be.

Moving on so I can wrap up this horrendously long stream of consciousness, I wake up every morning hating myself and finding myself wishing I could be proud of the young man I see in the mirror. I'm not some skeevy criminal or particularly horrible person, but I haven't been able to convince myself that I'm objectively a good person. I don't have a means of keeping myself accountable for my actions and decisions. I was never a religious person and have tried many times to no avail to try and discover my faith and spirituality.

Nihilism appealed to me at a young age because I arrogantly believed that there was nothing that could realistically exist that would be more powerful than my own discretion when determining my life choices. How could an entity have the means to control the direction of the world? I couldn't wrap my head around the idea that people worshipped beings they couldn't tangibly see or perceive. But maybe that wasn't necessary. Or even the point. As I matured I began to understand that sometimes people just need a reason to continue driving down life's convoluted roads. A reason that I felt I never had.

So, I started trying to find God in high school. I joined a bible study with some friends but was unable to commit myself to the scripture or beliefs. I felt like a pariah within a community centered around acceptance and inclusion. It was strangely hostile but not because of the people or the message; the feeling of being relegated to a lonely ghetto within my own soul made me feel threatened and belittled. I made empty prayers to a God I didn't believe in and picked up various religious texts in a desperate attempt to gain some insight into my spirit. My halfhearted ventures into religious faith all ended in abject fruitlessness which frustrated me and steered me closer towards existentialist void. Sounds pretty teen-angst edgy, I know, because that's exactly what it was.

Maybe the problem at heart was my attention was turned outwards when I needed to reflect introspectively. Rather than trying to place myself in the hands of someone I refused to believe in, there might be value in discovering faith in my own spirit. If I could find principle within my own soul perhaps I'd be able to move beyond hating myself all the time. How ironic that my biggest weakness could be my own inability to trust and believe in myself.

Furthermore, perhaps the underlying root cause of my struggles with spirituality stems from my lack of understanding of love. As I mentioned before, I never really felt as if I knew what love was growing up and I definitely didn't learn how to love from my parents or family. I've never been one to show affection and am terribly uncomfortable when receiving it. Sure, I write a lot about love but I honestly have never felt less acquainted than presently. One thing I know for certain is that learning to love myself and figuring out how to deal with my emotions is something I need to work on. I don't know how I'm going to do it and I don't know how long it will take, but I trust that I'll figure it out eventually. That's all I can really do at this point.

I'm not entirely sure why I just spilled my heart onto these pages. Maybe I cut my finger while typing and just desperately needed to bleed. Maybe it's a cry for help weaved into a dramatic personal narrative. If I had a blog I assume that'd be where this would best belong. But since that's just another place I can point people towards to not read my writing, you guys are stuck with this abomination of a pity party in this collection.

I guess I just wanted you guys to understand a little better what goes on in my head. I don't normally project much about myself outwardly but I guess this is what I tell people writing allows me to do. To be me is to be self-destructive and lost. There's nothing glamorous about being "Tyler Vo." I just hope I can survive being me.

Love

One of my absolute favorite topics to write about. I've most likely written at least fifty poems about love since I started seriously writing and probably even more unfinished bits and pieces. Unfortunately, like many of my earliest works, a good majority of them are lost whether it be because their only existence lay in the now wiped storage of old computers or I wrote them by hand in notebooks and loose scratch paper that have since been recycled. Or maybe that's a good thing because most of them were incredibly awkward and cringey. I was writing about love before I even had the smallest taste of it. Come to think of it, I definitely wrote many pieces about how I didn't know what love was as well. 15 year old me really thought he had the whole world figured out already. Luckily for everyone, he's an idiot and didn't; now I have an expansive collection of love poems I'm proud to vulnerably share with the world, including "Midnight on a Saturday."

(As a bonus, I included a poem I wrote when I was 15 adequately titled "a love poem" for reference)

Midnight on a Saturday

I always thought it best to let love come to me
And that I should accept the totality of its blessings and pain.
But I never knew how to explain what that love is supposed to feel like:
It's the way her smile lights up the entire city
It's the way she glides when she walks as if her footsteps are too pure for the Earth
It's the way her little laugh echoes down my spine, bringing joy to my every fiber
It's the way her hands fit in mine just perfectly
It's the way she likes to sit and talk for hours until there's not enough oxygen left in the room
It's the way she looks at me with her shimmering green eyes when I get excited
It's the way she sees me.
Reserved but expressive,
Intense but vulnerable,
Stoic but passionate,
Damaged but not broken,
Emotional but not quite tragic,
Flawed, but worth it.
The way she opens me up when I don't want to be read
Liberates my guarded heart, allowing me to be honest with myself.
I catch myself smiling stupidly at her right before she notices—
A small secret I hope to one day show her.
I feel comfortable and at ease as if her presence is enough reassurance
That although terror occupies my mind at night
She is the day that will save me from the darkness.
The gentle softness in her voice when she says 'I love you'

Sets the hills on fire and drains the oceans and
topples the mountains and blows away the sands of
the desert and knocks down the trees in the forest
and pulls the moon right from the sky,
Clearing the canvas for us to create our own world.
It's the way I've always seen her.
Delicate yet resilient,
Brilliant yet silly,
Cheerful yet haunted,
Mysterious yet familiar,
Beautiful yet scarred,
Lovely and wonderful as can be.

It's not entirely true that I never knew what love
meant to me
I lost myself searching for the right variance of love
that fit
And I let my heart bleed for something I thought I
wanted,
But now it's clear to me that it's her.
It's always been [the rest of the poem has been
redacted].

a love poem

I don't know what the breathtaking and beautiful
feeling of love feels like to its whole extent
But I feel as if I've had just a small taste of it
Just enough for me to know what my perfect kind of
love is:
- I want the type of love that makes you stutter when
you're talking and trip when you're walking just
thinking of how beautiful that love is
- I want the type of love where you smile for no
reason because you're in love kind of love
- When you fall asleep in your dreams because
you're so tired from being in love kind of love
- A love that moves mountains in your life to create
space for your love kind of love
- I want the type of love that will make me
reconsider how much I am in love just to remind me
that love is not defined by quality or reasons but
how strong the passion burns in your heart
- I want a love that knocks you down and then picks
you up just to knock you down again kind of love
- Because I want it all.
- I want the blissfully blind love that makes your
heart strum melodies so sweet and tender your mind
melts away to the harmonies of your heart
- I want the cold, uninviting loneliness of love when
you're separated from it for too long
- I want the bitter, gripping taste of love destroying
everything around you just to start over more
happily and content than before
- I want the deadly, sharp pain of a broken love that
haunts you, plaguing your thoughts with distant and
fading memories
- I want that love that makes you lose sanity and
control over your life

- I want the type of love that makes everything make sense
- I want the type of love that shakes the ground your heart treads on so violently that it summons a typhoon of despair and pain crashing through your brain in wake of a sandstorm of choking distaste followed by a piercing snowstorm that bombards your thoughts with ice-cold shards of doubt only to be welcomed by serene sunlight and joyful warmth
- I want my love to be a beautiful disaster.
- I want love to ruin my life so perfectly that my mind, heart, and soul come together to devote all of me to that love
- I want my love to obliterate my sanity so passionately and gently that I no longer think straight but solely out of romantic adoration
- I want my love to corrupt my thoughts with its sickeningly tender and affectionate grip
- I want my love to confuse me completely
And I'll be okay with it because a tragically beautiful love is what I've always wanted.

Danger

Danger is one of those sensations which, although I would primarily describe it as negative, tends to propel us forward and often times heightens our abilities and cognizance. There's a certain element of nervous energy that accompanies the most dangerous situations we find ourselves in. That combination of fear and adrenaline is what I sought to capture in *Rogue Timeline*. Personally, I find danger to be so compelling and intriguing, albeit something I don't actively seek at all times. Being able to put one's life on a balance and be tasked with meticulously deciding which way the scale tips is both a horrifying and gratifying experience. It allows us to assume control of our destiny in the most extreme scenario. And don't we all want to take the reins at some point? I chose to write about danger for one of the entries in the Red Collection because I associate danger with a superficial reddening of the senses, if you will. Our hearts beat faster, our minds narrow, the area around our vision turns a bit red, it might get a little warm. Those bodily responses as well as ideas such as code red and red alert. As you dive into Grace's world, try to pick up on the different senses of danger that you identify with and as always, enjoy.

Rogue Timeline

Grace stood cautiously over the strange
unmarked package at her doorstep. She peered
down both sides of the hallway quickly but saw
nothing. Slowly, she reached down and picked
the brown cardboard box up and retreated into
her apartment. Setting the box down on her
kitchen table, Grace continued to stare at the
package with unease. Her thoughts scrambled
but deep within her subconscious she knew the
immediate consequences that would ensue the
moment she was to open up Pandora's delivery.
With an exasperated sigh, Grace pulled her knife
off her waistband and cut the tape lining the
box.

Inside the box was a grey briefcase that opened
automatically once exposed to the dim kitchen
lights. A satellite phone and a small vial
containing pink fluorescent liquid revealed
themselves. Almost instinctively, Grace ran her
fingers around the edges of the briefcase,

searching for booby traps and hidden compartments. She noticed a small slit cut into the padding in one of the corners and dug her finger into the hole where she found a miniscule latch installed. Tugging on the latch triggered a holographic note in between the two contents of the briefcase. A single date was projected in red light.

"8.14 | 19:00"

That was in three days. Grace ran her fingers through her short brown hair and clasped them behind her head. She watched the projection disappear and looked down at her gifts. She grabbed the phone and turned it over. Inscribed on the lower register of the phone read:

"Don't ignore me. 5 minutes."

Immediately, her hand shot down under the kitchen table and removed the handgun strapped to the bottom. She aimed the gun steadily at the front door and eased her breathing, lowering her bionic heart rate to only generate 200 beats while she awaited her uninvited guest. Her body shook just slightly but her hands remained steadfast with her finger on the trigger.

300 seconds later and no sooner, two heavy knocks rapped on the front door. Inhaling a heavy gust of air, Grace slowly approached the door, keeping her gaze and weapon aimed directly at the forehead of her target behind the barrier.

"Let me in, Grace. I'm unarmed."

Grace turned the handle and yanked the door open, pressing the barrel of the gun onto the crown of her visitor's crouched head. A look of disbelief masked her face as she quickly lowered her gun to the ground.

"Michael? What the hell are you doing here?"

"Jesus Christ, Grace. No need for such

formalities, huh?"

Michael chuckled as he walked past Grace, grazing her shoulder as he let himself into her flat. Grace stood at the door, mouth agape, at a complete loss of words. She remained standing with the door open, gun in hand, while Michael sat himself down on the couch in the living room.

"You gonna join me? Or are you just gonna stand there and let a draft in?"

Grace closed the door and turned around to face her mentor. Her finger lay still on the trigger but her grip on the gun was relaxed. She stood motionless while allowing herself to regain her thoughts and composure. Her heart rate had risen slightly over 50 beats per minute, but she knew her body could not produce adrenaline: her body was simply gearing itself for combat by increasing blood flow to her brain.

"So, have you been able to settle in? How are

you liking it in the city?"

Michael broke the tense silence after a couple minutes. He scanned the rest of the apartment silently while waiting for Grace to answer. The décor was intentionally minimal and there was no indication that anybody was currently occupying the flat. Michael would have been correct in his assumption that the kitchen drawers were empty with the exception of an expansive selection of pristine cutlery. What Michael could verify, however, was that he was currently sitting on a weight sensitive explosive sewn into the couch, a tactical decision he made when he entered Grace's home.

"Damn I haven't seen you in who knows how long, and you can't even say hello? All I got was a gun to my head. Not really the warmest welcome for the man who brought you into the family and had your back since the beginning, you know."

"You didn't come here to talk, Michael. We both

44

know that you know I have no idea why you're here so can you please enlighten me? What's going on here?"

Grace squeezed the handle of the handgun harder as she stared impatiently at Michael from across the room. Her mechanically constructed muscles tightened while she ran her finger up and down the trigger.

With an exasperated sigh, Michael began to explain the purpose of his sudden visit:

"I wanted to be the person to tell you this because I know you and I know you won't be very happy about it, but you have to understand that this goes beyond me or anything in my control. They didn't even give me a reason or basis on which they made the final decision…

"You're expired, Grace. The Directors reviewed your most recent operation and reached the conclusion a few nights ago. I wish I could tell you why they decided to go about it this way, but they refused to let me see the case files. Which is strange because when I was assigned to be your mentor they couldn't move forward with any of your training modules until they received my final authorization. I'm not sure why they didn't consult me before making this decision. Now, I need you to stay calm while I explain to you the next steps in the--"

"They're gonna kill me. I already know..." Grace's voice trembled as its sound trailed off into the open air. Her mind overloaded with frenzied thoughts and processes, ultimately shutting her down as she collapsed to the ground in a cold sweat. She buried her head in her hands, struggling to comprehend the weight of Michael's words. The word 'expired' rang through her head incessantly like a broken record.

Is this really the end? What did I do wrong? Or is this some kind of test...?

Suddenly, Grace sprang to her feet and once

again aimed her gun at Michael's face. Her fear from moments earlier was instantaneously replaced with an aggressive squint that pierced through Michael's frank countenance. Without so much of a flinch, Michael raised his arms defiantly in maintenance of his innocence in the ordeal and shrugged his shoulders.

"There's no use in shooting me right here, Grace. If I wanted to die in this room I would have stood up five minutes ago. I know you've rigged this couch. That's precisely why I sat down here. I needed you to know that I'm not responsible for what the Directors decided. Hell, they don't even know I'm here right now. I switched out the sat phone with one of my personal burners to get the note to you. But I need you to calm down right now, put the gun away, and listen to me."

Grace obliged hesitantly and lowered her pistol to the ground. She floated over to the kitchen and sat down on the edge of the table. Her eyes dragged to the floor where she waited patiently for Michael to say his piece.

"At the exact date and time sent to you in the briefcase, you are going to hear a knock at the door. If you open that door, you will die. If you try to run before then, we will both die. That pink vial next to the sat phone? That preserves your previous prototype's existence in this present timeline."

This wasn't Michael's first time delivering a rendition of this speech. He paused intentionally to gauge Grace's reaction to everything he just told her. His lower lip quivered for a fleeting moment as he marveled despondently at his proudest creation. She remained quiet and composed and hadn't moved at all. Her eyes dug deeper into the floorboards as she silently pondered Michael's words.

Previous prototype. Present timeline. Timeline? Is he talking about time travel? And my previous prototype? I never made anything...or anyone. All I know is that vial seems like a death wish. I am definitely not drinking that stuff.

"Previous timeline? What are you talking about? Time travel? And I never made any prototypes."

Michael tried his best to offer a simple explanation of the Agency's history.

"During the earliest days of the Agency's conception, one of the founding Directors successfully developed previously unapproved time travel technology that would allow the Agency to operate across a multitude of timelines. However, due to government regulations preventing the use of time travel with humans, the Directors discovered a loophole which combined their newly patented cyborg operatives with the new technology. Since then, we've been using operatives of the same build, prototypes if you will, simultaneously with previous renditions occupying the past.

"You didn't make any. But I did in another

timeline many years ago. You see Grace, when one of our operatives expires, its most recent existing prototype succeeds it unless there is a presently built prototype ready to be implemented with functionality. That way, there is always a version of the operative in the current timeline. So, in order to prevent your entire existence from ending across all timelines in three days, inject the contents of that vial into your right arm. This will allow your previous prototype to assume your position in this timeline."

"Once it's done killing me. Got it. You want me to inject that stuff into my arm so that I can be... replaced? By some older version of me that you made in another lifetime? What the hell are you talking about Michael? This is ridiculous."

It became glaringly obvious to Grace that a final verdict had been reached and any attempt to reason with Michael would be ultimately fruitless. Her mind struggled to comprehend everything Michael had just said. She was programmed to understand dying and its nature but her emotional responses were not developed to react humanly to certain phenomena, death included. She learned to survive rather than live and now she had just been told there was no escaping her imminent fate in just a few days' time.

"Why are you telling me all of this? You said they don't know you're here. Why are you risking your life to warn me ahead of time?"

"Because I failed you, Grace. When I created you in the Lab, I implemented an operating system still in its trial phase that would allow me to teach you to learn human emotions. For many years, I've been advocating for the advancement of technology that would allow our operatives to be more human. I argued that making you guys more human would prevent mistakes in the event of crises or adaptive thinking. The machinated cyborgs can't react intuitively to new developments in the mission because they have none. However, the Directors delayed funding the project because they wanted complete control over the scripts and manufacture of our operatives. At the time you were built, I had a friend I trusted in the Lab upload the beta OS into your software. I held my breath throughout all your preliminary trainings and cognitive aptitude tests but was pleasantly surprised when you passed without any hiccups. They would have killed me if they found the altered code."

"So you gave me human emotions? The other operatives I worked with on my first mission couldn't think and feel the way I did? Why did you do that? Why did you have to complicate my life? Regardless, I don't understand what any of this has to do with me expiring for whatever reason in three days, Michael."

"It matters because you don't have to accept your fate… You're not a robot, Grace. You're just as much human as you are machine. Now I'm not telling you to run away because that won't work but I trust that you will think about what I told you today and discover what you want to do. But you have a choice in how you want to confront this. The other operatives? They don't have the chance to write their own ending. They'd just shut themselves down until their past comes to murder them."

The two old friends sat in silence for a while as Grace contemplated her course of action in utter distress. Her countenance revealed nothing of the internal battle waging in her core. Michael looked onward at Grace quietly as a few heavy tears escaped from his eyes only to be brushed off quickly accompanied by a subtle sniffle. Suddenly, Grace walked over to the couch and revealed a control panel projected onto the wall adjacent to the couch where Michael sat. She disarmed the IED beneath the seat cushions; Michael waited for the red warning signal to turn off on the panel before he placed his hands on his knees and slowly rose to his feet. The two looked at each other in melancholy reverence and engaged in a brief warm embrace before Michael turned towards the door and walked out.

What Grace didn't know and had no way of understanding was that Michael had come to love Grace like his own daughter. He watched her mature as an agent and her emotions felt so very real to him. Nonetheless, the very thing he fell in love with, the product of his rash decision to implement human emotion behind the Directors' backs, is what doomed Grace to her early retirement. Her feelings and minor quirks that differentiated her from his previous pupils captivated him and their relationship provided him with the meaningful filial interaction he was barred from having as an agent and mentor. Perhaps that was why he wanted to develop the code in the first place. He longed to feel the heartbeat of someone important to him who he cared about. Or maybe he wanted to experiment and advance the capabilities of the agency's operatives. That would have made him irreplaceable within the organizational ranks and surely would have given him more authority.

Regardless of his intentions, Michael made the critical error of allowing himself to become attached to his own operative. His mistakes came collecting and the first of his debts had been paid to the Directors on his behalf by his friend Romero from the Lab. Michael visited the Lab a week earlier to discuss an update for future renditions of the OS with Romero but was turned away by security without any concrete reason. Perplexed by the strange denial of entry, Michael called Romero on his personal cellphone but the number had been disconnected and he wasn't able to reach him on his agency phone either. Fearing the worst, Michael hurriedly drove to Romero's residence and was welcomed by the abject horror of his friend's dead body lying face down in a dried pool of dark blood in the middle of the kitchen. Cautiously, with tears swelling in his eyes, Michael approached Romero's body and turned it over.

Jesus Christ. What did they do to you, Romero? I'm so sorry…

It was clear that some sort of interrogation had taken place resulting in Romero's face having been beaten to disfiguration. Aside from the plethora of cuts and bruises marring Romero's face, what compelled Michael to fall to his knees in a wailing sob were the two scars on the sides of Romero's mouth. Michael placed his trembling hands on his friend's lips and pulled them open to read the Directors' message: Romero's tongue had been cut out and shoved into a hole drilled into his throat. The Directors clearly wanted whoever found the body to know that they had figured out Romero was developing rogue operating systems with the intention of hidden implementation into operatives. Fearing he was being monitored, Michael placed Romero's body back to its original position and quickly left.

He returned to the agency and devised his plan to warn Grace. Her mission debriefing was scheduled for the next day and he knew that he needed to get access to her retirement package before it was sent in order to switch sat phones. There was also no way for him to determine if the Directors knew Romero was working with somebody else from within the organization without stirring up unwanted attention. Thus, Michael had to remain calm and proceed with his obligations as routinely as possible.

At Grace's mission debriefing, the Directors analyzed the footage from Grace's bodysuit and retinal cameras and began taking notes on the successes and shortcomings of the mission. Michael watched as the Directors pointed out her precision with the long gun while providing overhead support for the ground team. They noted that her marksmanship training was top of her class and had placed her in the elite squad. Michael zoned in and out of the meeting while maintaining his focused gaze on the briefcase at the end of the table. How was he going to have unsupervised access to the briefcase without arousing suspicion? Protocol dictated that the mentor of an expired operative could only provide a recommendation for the expiration date and would then leave the room while the Directors discussed other parameters related to reassignment and relocation.

Michael's attention reverted to the meeting at hand when a hushed silence suddenly fell over the room. He looked up at the screen and saw the footage rewinding.

"Stop. Right there. Did you see how she hesitated when her eyes locked onto the target? What the hell happened there?"

"She froze up when she saw a child crouched behind the woman with the rifle. She didn't pull the trigger."

The Directors muttered excitedly amongst themselves as they tried to understand what compelled Grace to stall on a routine shot. Was it a glitch? There's no reason why an operative would not immediately fire on an armed insurgent when providing support.

In the video, Michael noticed the woman was trembling as she was most likely scared and had no choice but to try and defend herself. Grace must have noticed that she was simply protecting her daughter. He watched as Grace fired just wide to the right of the woman, ultimately missing her, sending the woman and her daughter running out of the camera's view. Moments later, a loud explosion erupted and collapsed the roof where the mother and daughter were just standing on seconds ago.

"Wait. She... saved their lives? What the fuck is going on here? There's no way she missed a point blank shot like that. She finished training with record marks in mid-range precision!"

The Directors were infuriated. Black flag missions were reserved for the most trusted and decorated operatives, none of which carried a history of malfunctions. It soon became obvious to the Directors that Grace's OS had been corrupted and she could no longer be treated as a secure asset.

Michael began to sweat. Prior to the debriefing, he was not given any indication as to what warranted the decision to expire Grace. Now, he saw the exact moment when Grace's humanity exposed her to the Directors outright. There was no escaping this one. Michael knew that the investigation into Romero's treason would conclude very soon that he had been working with others. And now that Grace's erroneous mission revealed human-like behavior, it was only a short matter of time before the Directors parsed through Romero's beta and matched its scripts to Grace's deviance. Pinning Romero's crime to Grace would inevitably link Michael to the investigation, in which case he would be killed as soon as the target was painted on his back.

After just over three hours had passed, the Directors summoned Michael over to the front of the table in order to program the briefcase for its delivery date. He walked deliberately and slightly hesitantly so he could scan the room and choose his window to cause a minor distraction that would allow him to slip his personal sat phone, which was secured in a harness on the underside of his forearm, into the briefcase while grabbing the one assigned to Grace. Michael began searching up Grace's various residences and pretended to ponder each location before choosing the flat he already knew she was staying at. Taking one last register of the room, he saw that most of the Directors weren't paying any attention to him. Just as he finished typing in the address and desired day of delivery, he lifted the sat phone in the briefcase and released the one in the harness. He made sure to lift the phone with his hands on top of the phone and angled his arm so the replacement would slide in perfectly while instantly pushing the original sat phone right back into his sleeve. Michael turned to the Director closest to him and nodded his approval that the briefcase was ready for delivery.

Over the next couple of days, Michael slept restlessly and sporadically as he struggled to cope with the imminent fate awaiting Grace and, most likely, him as well. He was only partially concerned with his own wellbeing. The fact that he had created Grace to be emotionally human meant that he owed it to her to provide an explanation. Typically, operatives merely shut themselves down and await the arrival of their past to kill them. Grace wouldn't do that. The thought of her blank confusion and distress rattled Michael and kept his thoughts stampeding through his mind at night. With that, he decided to meet Grace at her apartment the day of the package delivery.

Once Michael left her flat, Grace fell down onto her couch and placed her head in her hands as she stared dumbfoundedly at the ground. Her green eyes blinked mechanically while she pondered everything she was just told.

I'm… human? I'm like Michael? The other operatives are different, he said. I'm going to die in three days.

Three days. Was she supposed to prepare

somehow for this once in a lifetime encounter with the past version of herself? At first, Grace thought to arm her apartment to the teeth with various traps that would at least give her a fighting chance against whatever was about to visit her. She activated her explosives and sensors and sat in her kitchen on the floor behind the counter with a semi-automatic rifle lying on the ground next to her and a pistol in her hand. She sat there unwaveringly and intensely for 24 hours without moving, her finger grazing the edge of the trigger. She waited as patiently as someone could when facing inevitable death. But her stillness abruptly subsided and she stood up quickly, tucking the pistol back into the back of her pants.

Grace walked back into her living room and stood over the expiration briefcase. She picked up the sat phone and thought briefly about calling Michael. No. She couldn't put him in any more danger than he was already in. She held the glowing pink vial up to the light and studied its contents. The liquid was completely flat and clear without a single bubble or particle floating around. Grace didn't even have a needle lying around to inject the contents of the vial into her right arm like Michael had said. Over the next few hours, Grace sat at her dining table and stared timidly at the briefcase. Her mind roamed as she sifted through half-assed plans ranging from fleeing to standing her ground and fighting. Michael had previously warned her of the futility of trying to escape, but regardless of how protected she could outfit her apartment to be, being a sitting duck didn't provide much sense of security either.

What if she were able to kill her past? What happens then? Surely, the Directors would find out and Grace had very little confidence she'd be able to last more than a few hours before the agency captured her. At that point, they'd probably brutalize and torture her before either shutting her down or simply killing her. No matter how fruitless or awful the probable outcomes of her various options seemed, Grace could not convince herself to let herself die.

Maybe that was the human emotion in her. Or maybe she refused to let the Directors control her fate. Whichever it was, she was determined to meet her past face to face.

August 14th came around and Grace tried her best to prepare herself for a shootout with her past. Her hidden pistols were placed in their usual locations behind walls and underneath furniture. The rest of the additions to her home security included: reinforced steel bars spread across the front door, a motion detected tranquilizer dart roughly five feet past the entrance, and a long gun installed in the kitchen with a firing timer aimed through the wall such that the trigger would pull at the exact moment her target begins to collapse from the tranquilizer. Not wanting to risk direct combat with her past, Grace evacuated her neighbors across the hall and positioned herself just behind the wall by the front door of their apartment. She kept two handguns on her waist, only willing to reveal herself if her target were to somehow survive her trap. It was here that she remained crouched, sweat just slightly dropping from her forehead as she placed her ear to the wall, listening keenly for footsteps in the hallway.

After some time waiting, Grace heard the door to the stairwell swing open and a flurry of stumbling footsteps rumbled down the hall. She pressed her head into the wall, making sure not to miss a sound. She glanced down at her watch. 18:52. A small smirk began to form across her lips as Grace reveled in the thought that the Directors had sent her past with ample time for a fight, yet there would be none. The steps halted just in front of her opposite the wall. Something thudded loudly against the door to her apartment, followed by a series of beeps. An explosive breach.

Clever, but still won't save you.

Within seconds, a loud explosion violently shook the walls of the room and the ground beneath Grace. She could hear rubble being moved as deliberate footsteps entered her apartment. Her grip on the pistol hardened intensely. Then, a soft thud came from a few feet inside the door. Her plan worked. Grace rose to her feet slowly, drawing both guns and quietly walked out from across the hallway. Her gaze remained fixed on the collapsed pile of steel and drywall as dust continued to float over the mess. As she approached the destruction and entered the doorway, she looked down and saw the dead body on the ground. When the dust settled, the outline and figure of the corpse revealed itself to be a larger man dressed in ordinary clothes. A growing pool of blood pouring out from beneath the body seeped onto her boots as Grace stood frozen in her tracks. Instinctively, she turned her focus towards the wall bordering the kitchen, behind which she hid her sniper rifle. She fired off six shots, three from each gun, at the wall but heard nothing.

Suddenly, the body by her feet shifted and an arm shot up with a needle clasped in its hand. The man stabbed the needle into Grace's right arm and injected the pink liquid inside. Before she could realize what was going on, the man's other arm grabbed onto Grace's hand and tried dragging her down. The two struggled briefly before Grace pointed the gun at the man's chest and sent two piercing bullets through his heart. His body dropped heavily as his lifeless hands fell from her arms and legs.

Dazed and confused, Grace stood up and began walking uneasily towards the kitchen. She only took two steps before a muzzled bark escaped from the kitchen, letting out a 20mm long missile dressed in a sleek copper jacket launched by the fiery spark of a hammer. A hole 9mm wide punched its way through the kitchen wall and continued straight through the back of Grace's throat, simultaneously ripping her esophagus and shattering her vertebrae. With quickly expiring consciousness, Grace fell to the floor clumsily and began convulsing as the sanguine fluid choked her and spilled out from her neck, soaking her hair and torso. Her body struggled to allow her to die like so for a few more seconds before succumbing to the grip of fate right there on the cold wooden floor.

Out from the dark, shadowy recess of the kitchen walked a large man wearing a blue coat and low-brimmed baseball cap. He pulled out a sat phone and dialed the only number on the phone's call list.

"Yeah, I got her. Clean shot right in the neck. She set up a few traps as expected but I did a clean scan of the place before I went in. Yeah, we got her in the arm with the vial. She believed in the past prototype bullshit."

He walked out into the living room to inspect Grace's body and confirm her death. Lying there in the dim afternoon sunset was Grace's pale body, completely covered in the crimson blood as if it were painted. The man withheld a whimper of mixed disgust and agony as he continued staring at the macabre scene he created.

On the other end of the line there was a gruff

voice speaking.

"Excellent job, Michael. I'm sorry for your loss. You did well. The Directors thank you for your service."

Once Michael heard those last seven words, he dropped the phone and began frantically unbuttoning his coat to reveal a string of explosives strapped onto the vest he was wearing. His other hand was occupied with holding down a dead man's switch while he furiously fumbled with the controls of the detonator, trying desperately to open circuit the board and defuse the seismic bomb attached to his waist. His training as an aspiring operative many years ago served him well as he easily recalled the steps taught to him for disarming explosives. Working with only one hand greatly slowed him down but he knew that he only had five minutes to disarm the bomb once it had been activated. He figured the Directors armed the explosives once he was able to confirm that he had successfully killed Grace and he was right. However, what he was not aware of was a manual lockout failsafe that was installed into the motherboard of the detonator that would prevent Michael from completing the disarmament in its entirety.

Michael's speed and acumen betrayed him when the detonator spontaneously shut off after he identified the inputs to the first regulator on the board and successfully removed them without trouble. Perspiration began to seep to the surface of his fingertips as he wildly tugged at wires and pressed buttons to no avail. He was locked out.

No, no, no. This can't be happening. What the hell? Did I mess up? There's no way. I definitely didn't forget the first few steps.

Tears streamed down his face as Michael finally realized there was no escaping his death sentence. Deep down he knew when he woke up in the mission briefing room donning a suicide vest after being kidnapped from his own house that the Directors had discovered the truth and could not afford to let him live. They told him he could redeem himself and prove himself trustworthy again if he went and killed Grace himself. The vest was just for collateral, they said. In the moment, he told himself their word meant something, even if just for a miniscule fragment of hope. So, he went home and drank himself into a barely manageable stupor as the clock trudged through every devastating minute towards 19:00.

When he got to Grace's apartment building, he was greeted by the doorman, who by now was an Agency operative, and escorted to her apartment. In order to not scare off Grace with the obvious sound of multiple people's footsteps, Michael stumbled through the hallway, bumping into the walls every now and then to create enough noise to mask the sound of the Agency operative crawling on the ground beside him. After they breached the front door, Michael shoved the other operative to the ground from behind in order to avoid triggering the tranquilizer. To his greater fortune, Michael's companion had knocked himself unconscious when he hit his head on a large chunk of rock when he fell to the ground. Quickly, Michael disabled the tranquilizer and waltzed into the kitchen and assumed his position behind the long gun just beneath the counter it was sitting on. He did not quite anticipate the operative waking up while Grace was standing over him, but their struggle gave Michael the confidence that Grace was perfectly in line with the rifle's aim. All he had to do was pull the trigger, which he did with two steps' hesitation.

Now, as he stood over her frail corpse with her blood on his hands, Michael realized the cruel irony in his punishment. Although there was no reality in Michael living beyond the night, the Directors forced his hand and ultimately made him kill his own creation. They told him to recite the same scripted expiration speech to Grace about her past prototypes that he has told various times to his other mentees. Except those operatives actually had existing prototypes ready to enter this timeline. Michael knew damn well Grace was the first prototype in her line and the Directors figured it would be poetic justice for Michael to be the one that pulled the trigger. Michael was literally Grace's only past, and indeed her past arrived on August 14th to kill her.

Michael let out an agonizing scream as he ripped off the tape holding his finger down on the dead man's switch. He closed his eyes and braced for the momentary impact of the explosives but nothing happened. He yelled in frustration as he could not even voluntarily detonate the bomb. The window shattered as a distant firework cracked and an explosive round met its target on Michael's waistband. As a single tear made its way towards Grace's pool of blood on the ground, Michael watched as each bundle of C4 on his chest exploded in quick succession, instantaneously ripping him apart and obliterating the apartment building's fourth floor and beyond. As the tremors made their way through the building's central structural support, fires erupted along every internal fiber,

---

eventually toppling the entire compound into a gargantuan pile of rubble and dust.

"Did you get him?"

A voice coupled with radio static echoed into an earpiece on a rooftop 3000m away.

"Yeah, I hit the C4. Whole building's razed. Yeah, there's nothing left."

A slender, handsome young man stood over the edge of a high rise building gripping the smoking long gun. He grimaced as his eye took stock of the destruction he just caused through the scope of the rifle. His mind drifted to the hundreds of innocent lives he just murdered by detonating the C4 and dropping the entire apartment complex. Nothing beyond a calculation of lives weighed against the scope of the mission crossed his mind as he callously switched his focus back to packing up his gear and returning to the extraction point. The radio in his earpiece crackled to life once again as he took apart his rifle.

"Good job, Michael. The Directors thank you for your service."

With the death sentence parlayed, Michael inhaled one last breath of air before his body spontaneously combusted, dismembering and spraying his body in every direction across the rooftop like paint splattered on a barren canvas.

Rose

The rose is a quintessential symbol of love and romance, both the beauty and pain. Its thorns have played a significant role in its depiction throughout history and I've always been fascinated with them. I am particularly drawn to the idea of something so beautiful and desired, but if not handled carefully is capable of hurt. Furthermore, when it comes to the rose, I'm less concerned with its traditional symbolism as I am with its growth. A blossoming flower encapsulates hope and positivity in the exact manner I envision innocent optimism to be portrayed. Maybe it's just the romantic in me but I find the sprouting of petals on newly budding flowers to be extremely moving. It's one of my proudest works, so I hope you find "petals" as beautiful as a rose.

petals

In a garden underneath the pouring rain a rose
struggles to keep its breath,
Drowning beneath the never ending droplets from
above.
Small flowing streams flush away the dirt deposits
covering its neighbors
While simultaneously crashing into its stem,
Pulling it towards the gutter and tempting its roots
to let go of their grasp on the Earth.
Water drips from the leaves once they succumb to
the weight of holding up the world
On their shoulders, relieving the rose of its past
As Poseidon's rage continues to heave wet tipped
spears down from the Heavens.
It was only a few days ago that our rose poked its
head out from under the ground
How did we get here so quickly?
We went from celebrating the budding start of our
growth
To counting the petals that have fallen,
Tearing themselves on every thorn on the way down
Just to be swept away with the remnants of our
memories.
Tell me that the sun will rise again and banish the
darkness to obscurity;
Show me the truth behind the curses you have cast
on our efflorescence;
Make me believe that we were never more than an
accident;
Prove to me that the seeds we planted will never
amount to anything
Beyond a midsummer miracle;
Because I'm getting really tired of playing she loves
me, she loves me not
While I stare hopelessly at our petals as we wither
and rot.

Warmth

It's when every fiber of your body tingles with the creeping sensation of security and assurance. You can feel your skin opening up and relaxing. Whether it be from the fiery rays of our heavenly star or the comfort of a soft blanket or something in between, the incredible feeling remains the same. That immediate gratification when you strive for so long to escape the bitter cold and enter the confines of a car with the heater blasting or a cozy cabin bearing the weight of heavy snow on its rooftop. How your face flushes and you try to hide the redness as your senses falter just a little and everything from your cheeks to your ears become flustered when your love looks into your eyes and smiles. It's the way everything feels right in the world if just for a moment in time. Hold on to these flashes of warmth and capture them near to your heart. You'll never know when the day will come again when you find yourself entangled in the night and the sun's brilliant light arrives just in time to save you.

Day

The sun hasn't come out in years
But the inevitable cold has dimly faded,
Giving way to a slowly encroaching wave of warmth:
A tingling sensation creeping through your veins
slowly
And awakening hibernated thoughts and harbored
emotions.

She's the sunrise that (jump) starts my every day
And I've been unconscious longer than I can
remember.
My heart has atrophied, rendering my blood placid
and still.
Darkness has more than blinded my vision
It clouds my mind with shivering doubt
As I lie awake through the everlasting night.

The moon disappeared from orbit in my past life,
Leaving me without a glimpse of direction in the
night sky.
I yearn to wake up to her radiating glow by my side
But she only flashes her breathtaking smile to the
other side of the world
Thousands of miles into the future where my arms
only hope to reach.
It's the allure of possibility that keeps me alive
Waiting impatiently for her to turn her devoted
affection towards
My crippled, callous garden
Trampled and trounced by gale force heartbreak.
My tulips have started to drown from the morphine
drip
That numbs my frail vulnerability.

I need her warm glow to illuminate my life so my future's present can become my past and our present's future can blossom into the final chapter of my story.
Until then, my book remains stranded in time on an empty canvas
Lest I see another day.

Made in the USA
Las Vegas, NV
01 April 2025

20325241R00052